AKIMBO
AND THE
BABOONS

Alexander McCall Smith lives in
Scotland. He likes writing about Africa,
where he spent his childhood. He is
married to a doctor and they have two
daughters, Lucy and Emily. His hobbies
are playing music on wind instruments
and sailing.

Also by Alexander McCall Smith

Akimbo and the Elephants
Akimbo and the Crocodile Man
Akimbo and the Lions
Akimbo and the Snakes

The Bubblegum Tree
The Doughnut Ring
The Popcorn Pirates
The Spaghetti Tangle
The Banana Machine
The Joke Machine
The Muscle Machine
Calculator Annie
Teacher Trouble

The Chocolate Money Mystery
The Bursting Balloons Mystery

The Five Lost Aunts of Harriet Bean
Harriet Bean and the League of Cheats
The Cowgirl Aunt of Harriet Bean

AKIMBO
AND THE
BABOONS

ALEXANDER McCALL SMITH

Illustrated by Peter Bailey

BLOOMSBURY
CHILDREN'S
BOOKS

First published in Great Britain in 2008 by Bloomsbury Publishing Plc
36 Soho Square, London, W1D 3QY

Text copyright © Alexander McCall Smith 2008
Illustrations copyright © Peter Bailey 2008
The moral rights of the author and illustrator have been asserted

A CIP catalogue record of this book is available from the British Library

ISBN 978 0 7475 9457 4

All papers used by Bloomsbury Publishing are natural, recyclable products
made from wood grown in well-managed forests. The manufacturing processes
conform to the environmental regulations of the country of origin.

Typeset by Dorchester Typesetting Group Ltd
Printed in Italy by Legoprint

1 3 5 7 9 10 8 6 4 2

www.mccallsmithbooks.co.uk
www.bloomsbury.com

Contents

Letter from the author

Special visitors   1

Into the bush   11

A close call   21

Lunchtime lesson   31

Tommy and Ben   43

Baboon rescue   51

Off track   63

Help!   73

Brilliant baboon facts   83

Dear Reader,

Some people think that baboons are not very nice. They say that they have ugly faces, are quarrelsome, and don't seem to like humans very much. While it is true that baboons are wary of people – and they often have good reason to be – it's certainly not fair to describe them as ugly and quarrelsome. The truth of the matter is that baboons are very interesting animals – rather closer in their behaviour to ourselves than we might like to admit!

I have often seen baboons on my trips to Africa. I am always pleased to come across them, as I enjoy watching them run along the side of the road or climb up on logs and trees to watch what's going on. Of course if you watch them for only a short time you never really find out much about them. To do that, you have to study them for weeks and months at a time.

On a recent trip to Botswana, I met people who had been watching baboons for many years.

They were scientists who eventually wrote a book about the baboons they had come to know so well. In this book, they described how baboons thought about the world, about how they had friends – and enemies – and how they organised the groups in which they lived.

This book is much shorter than that. But I hope that at the end of it you will know a little bit more about these amazing animals who, like us, just want to get on with their lives in peace.

With warmest wishes,

Alexander McCall Smith

Special visitors

There are some days that just feel exciting, right from the beginning, and this was one of them.

School had finished for the year and a whole month of doing exactly as he pleased stretched out in front of Akimbo. That was thrilling enough, but to make things better, this was the day that his cousin, Kosi, was due to arrive for a three week stay. He was the same age as Akimbo, or almost – Akimbo had been born two days before him, and that made a big difference, or so Akimbo sometimes said.

Kosi liked coming to stay with Akimbo. Not only were the two boys firm friends, but for Kosi, who lived in a town, it was a chance to stay on the great game reserve where Akimbo's father was head ranger. This was a real treat for him, and he always counted the days until his uncle, Akimbo's father, picked him up at the station in his truck.

So there was a lot of excitement that morning when Kosi arrived and carried his things into the room he was to share with Akimbo. But there was more to come.

'We're having another visitor today,' announced Akimbo's father. 'The baboon lady is arriving at lunchtime.'

Akimbo looked at his father. 'The baboon lady?' he asked. He had not heard of anybody called that before and he wondered what it meant. Was this a lady baboon? Or was it a woman who had a pet baboon?

His father saw Akimbo's puzzlement and

smiled. 'No,' he said, 'it's not a baboon. She's a scientist. She's one of these people who study baboons. And she knows a lot about them, I can tell you!'

Akimbo was a little bit disappointed. He liked baboons, who he thought were even cleverer than monkeys, and it would have been interesting to have a visiting baboon. He and Kosi could have played with him, he imagined, and if the baboon behaved well enough he might have been allowed to sit at the table while they had their meals. Now all he had to look forward to was a scientist.

'You'll like her,' his father went on. 'She's lived with baboons, you know. They treated her as another baboon.'

Kosi laughed. 'And did she eat what they ate?' he enquired.

'You ask her yourself,' said Akimbo's father. 'Ask her about it at lunch.'

The two boys had plenty to occupy themselves with that morning and lunchtime seemed to come round very quickly. They had seen no sign of the baboon lady, but when Akimbo's mother sent a message over to the ranger office that lunch was ready, the boys saw Akimbo's father walking over to the house with a tall woman carrying a satchel over her shoulder.

'My name is Jenny,' said the woman as she shook the boys' hands. 'But people often just call me Jen. So you can do that if you want to.'

Akimbo found himself liking Jen immediately. She had a warm smile which seemed to hover about her lips all the time, as if somebody had just said something funny, or was about to. And Akimbo could tell that Kosi liked her too.

He wondered what she was doing in the game reserve. Animal scientists often came to see his father, and they usually had some project or other that they wanted to do. Sometimes they just wanted to count a particular sort of animal. Sometimes they wanted to tag the animals and see where they migrated to. And sometimes they wanted to take blood samples, to send off to their

4

laboratories for testing. That was easy enough with some animals, but with others it involved putting the animal to sleep for a while with a special dart. That could be dangerous – not only for the animal, but also for the people who had to get close enough to fire the dart.

It became clear at lunchtime what Jen planned to do.

'Perhaps you could tell the boys what your plans are,' said Akimbo's father. 'I know that they're interested.'

'You're interested in baboons?' exclaimed Jen. 'Well, I'm not surprised, boys. They are very fascinating creatures. They're a lot like us, you know – like you and me.'

She began to explain what she was planning to do. With the agreement of Akimbo's father, his men had built a small hut for her in a part of the reserve where there was a large pack of baboons. Over the next two weeks, she was going to live out there, night and day, and while she was doing this she was going to watch the habits of the baboons.

'There's something I particularly want to find out,' Jen said. 'I want to see how they share their food.'

Akimbo looked surprised. He did not think that animals shared their food very much. He thought it was first come, first served.

'Do they really share?' he asked.

'Yes, they do,' said Jen. 'Not always, but a lot of the time. And that's something I've been studying.'

Kosi, who had been silent, now asked a question. 'Why?' he said.

Akimbo thought that was a rather simple question, but Jen took it seriously.

'I want to find out,' she said, 'because it helps us to understand how baboons see the world.'

The two boys thought about this for a

moment. Then Jen suddenly turned to Akimbo's mother and father.

'Would you let the boys come out to see what I do?' she asked. 'I'm sure that they'd enjoy it.'

Akimbo's father looked at his wife, who hesitated for a moment before she nodded. 'If they promise to behave themselves,' she began.

'They can be looked after by the junior ranger you were going to lend me as my assistant,' said Jen. 'I'm sure he'll watch the boys for you.'

Akimbo's father stared down at his plate. He looked embarrassed by something. 'Actually,' he began, 'there's a bit of a problem there. We're very short-handed at the ranger station, I'm afraid. Two of the men are off sick and so . . . Well, we won't be able to lend you an assistant after all.'

For a few moments nobody said anything. Then, quite unexpectedly, Akimbo broke the silence. 'We'll help,' he blurted out. 'Kosi and I can be your assistants, Jen. Please!'

Again there was silence. Now it was Akimbo's father's turn to speak. 'Well . . .' he began.

It seemed to Akimbo that his father was about to say no. But Jen did not understand it this way. 'Oh, thank you,' she said enthusiastically. 'They'll be very useful, and I'm sure that they'll be very careful, won't you, boys?'

Akimbo and Kosi both nodded vigorously. It was settled!

Into the bush

There was a lot to do that day if they were to be ready to leave the next morning. Jen had all the supplies with her that she would need for her time in the bush, but now that Akimbo and Kosi were to join her, more provisions were needed. Fortunately, Akimbo's mother's store cupboard was full, and she was able to come up with all the food and other things they would need.

'I've never been camping,' Kosi said to Akimbo. 'I can't wait to try it!'

Akimbo shared his cousin's enthusiasm. Of course he had spent a lot of time in the bush with his father, but this was a bit different. There would be no parents on this trip, and that made him feel very grown-up.

And there was another thing that made this trip special. Since they would be helping her, Jen had announced that she would pay the boys a small amount of money each day. This made Akimbo feel very important. He had always helped in the past without being paid, but this would be a real job.

The next morning, when the time came to leave, the two boys helped Jen load everything into her truck and secure it for the bumpy ride ahead. They would be travelling along rough tracks and they would have to make sure that nothing was damaged on the journey. Jen had some delicate equipment with her, including a telescope to watch the baboons with, and a large expensive camera. It was very important that all this was safe.

It took them five hours to reach the place where the hut had been built. They travelled through thick bush made up of tall grass and high trees, and at several points along the journey Jen

had to stop to
check up on
their position.
Then suddenly
Akimbo saw
the hut which
had been erected
not far from the
base of a huge
granite rock.

'There!' he shouted. 'That's the place.'

Jen turned the truck off the track and they
made the last of the bumpy journey through the
waist-high grass. It was like driving across the sea,
thought Akimbo, as he watched the grass part in
front of the truck.

They came to a halt beside the hut. It was not
much of a building – and you could easily miss it
if you weren't looking for it. It had been made out
of the branches of trees and the trunks of saplings,
all tied together with twine and then poked firmly
into the ground. There was a simple door, made

out of a sheet of thin wood, and a roof of bundles of thatch.

'Well,' said Jen, surveying their new home. 'At least we don't have to be here for long!'

For Akimbo and Kosi the hut was just right. Although it was dark inside – there were no windows to let in the light – it seemed comfortable enough. The floor was earth, pounded down to make it hard, and right in the middle a few stones had been stacked together to make a fireplace.

'It's perfect,' said Akimbo, laying his sleeping bag down on the floor. 'Can we make a fire?'

Jen suggested that they wait until the evening for that, but in preparation she set the boys to collecting firewood which they could use when the time came. Then they busied themselves with unpacking the rest of the equipment and setting up camp. At last, by mid-afternoon, everything was in place.

'Now what?' asked Akimbo. 'Do we go and find the baboons now?'

Jen shook her head. 'I think that the baboons

are more likely to find us,' she said. 'They live quite close by and they're very inquisitive creatures. So we'll just sit here and wait.'

'Won't they be frightened of us?' asked Kosi.

Jen explained that this was unlikely. 'These baboons have hardly ever seen human beings,' she said. 'They'll be careful, but they won't really be frightened of us. Animals that have never been harmed by human beings are often quite fearless.'

They waited for what seemed like a very long time. Akimbo found himself itching to get up and look around, but Jen had told them that they should all just stay quiet until something happened.

And then it did. The first sign was a barking sound from the direction of the hill. To begin with Akimbo thought it was a wild dog, but then Jen raised a finger, pointed into the long grass, and smiled expectantly. So it must be a baboon.

A few minutes later, while Akimbo was looking in quite the opposite direction, there was a sudden movement at the edge of the clearing.

Then, a few moments later, a dark shape emerged. It was the first of the baboons.

When the baboon saw Akimbo and the others sitting under

the tree beside the hut, he stopped where he was. Raising himself up on his hind legs he stared at the three strangers. Then he dropped back to his haunches and bared his teeth. They were large, discoloured teeth, like fangs, and Akimbo thought that he would not like to be bitten by a baboon.

'Just stay quite still,' whispered Jen. 'Let him get used to us.'

The baboon stared at them for a few moments and then disappeared back into the grass.

'He's gone,' said Kosi, sounding rather disappointed.

'Not for long,' whispered Jen. 'You'll see.'

She was right. A few minutes later, the large baboon reappeared. This time he was accompanied by several other members of the troop, including a female with a tiny baby baboon holding on to her. The baby was upside down, but seemed quite happy with the ride.

The baboons now sat down and stared back at the people. They were making low noises, little coughs and grunts, as if they were talking to one

17

another. Akimbo wondered what they could be saying, and if it was a special baboon language they were using. Or was it just noises?

While he was thinking this, Jen suddenly stood up. When the baboons saw her do this, they gave a start, but quickly settled down.

'You boys stand up too,' she said. 'Don't make any other movements. Just stand up.'

The two boys did as they were told, all the while being watched by the baboons with a mixture of wariness and curiosity. Then, after a couple of minutes, the first baboon gave a grunt and the whole group turned round and loped off into the grass again.

Jen looked at the boys, rubbing her hands together with satisfaction. She seemed very pleased.

'Good!' she said. 'They've taken a good look at us and they know about us. So tomorrow we can approach them and they won't be too worried.'

The boys had hoped to see more of the baboons, but at least this was a start. And there were things to do now – the fire to make, as it would soon become dark, and they would need to cook dinner. So everybody was busy for a while and had no time to think of the night ahead and what it might bring.

A close call

After they had finished their meal, Jen and the boys sat outside the entrance to the hut, listening to the sounds of the African night. In the background there was the chirrup of insects, a shrill sound that became louder and then softer in waves. Then, from time to time, there were other sounds – the shriek of a nocturnal bird of prey, the grunt of some creature scurrying its way through the undergrowth. The night was not quiet.

Nor was it dark. No sooner had the sun gone burning down than an almost-full moon floated up over the hills. This bathed the bush in a soft light that seemed to make the whole world a place of mysterious shapes and shadows. Was that a bush or an elephant? Of course it was just a bush, but had it not moved? Just the wind, said Jen. Just the wind.

After a while it was time to go to bed. They had all brought sleeping bags and had made beds for themselves out of grass and leaves. Akimbo put a couple of large logs on the fire that they had made in the centre of the hut, and this comforted them as they snuggled down into their sleeping bags.

'I hope there are no lions near here,' said Kosi, in a small voice. This was all very different from his room back in the town where he lived, and he was feeling a bit nervous.

'There are,' said Akimbo. 'But they won't come in here – the fire will keep them away. Don't worry.'

Kosi felt very frightened. He was glad, though, that he had his older cousin with him – and this really was one of those times when it mattered that Akimbo was two days older.

It was Akimbo who woke up first in the middle of the night. He was not sure what had awoken him, but it was certainly a noise of some sort. He wondered whether it was a lion, and he was relieved to see that the fire in the hut was still glowing strongly. He listened carefully.

He heard the noise again. This time it was

louder, and this time he knew exactly what it was. It was a baboon barking. And now there was more barking, louder and angrier than before. This time it woke Jen up, and then Kosi.

'What's going on?' Akimbo whispered.

'Something's happening at their sleeping place,' said Jen, rubbing the sleep out of her eyes.

'Can we go and see?' asked Akimbo.

Jen looked doubtful. You did not walk about the African bush at night unless you had a very good reason to do so. But now the baboons started to howl, and Jen got out of her sleeping bag.

'We can go and take a look,' she said. 'We'll take the flashlights.'

The boys slipped out of their sleeping bags and put on their shoes. As usual, Akimbo held his shoes upside down for a moment or two, just in case a scorpion had decided to make its bed in one of them. Then, walking in single file behind Jen, they began to make their way through the bush towards the sound of the distressed baboons.

The baboons slept between rocks at the foot of

the nearby granite hill. This was a good place for them, as they could tuck themselves away in little spaces and caves between the boulders, and this kept them warm and safe during the night. As they approached the rocks, Jen told the boys to turn off their flashlights so that they could observe what was happening without frightening the baboons even more.

At first, even in the moonlight, it was hard to make out which shadows were baboons and which were rocks. But then, as they crouched and stared at the scene, they were able to make out the shapes of the baboons and watch their movements.

A number of the baboons had climbed up on to the top of the boulders and were swaying around, howling and barking in alarm. Others were still in their little caves and were barking out from there, their voices echoing against the walls of rock.

'Something's really upsetting them,' whispered Jen. 'Something that . . .'

She did not finish. At that moment, Akimbo gave a cry and reached out to pull Jen to the ground. She had been crouching in front of him, and he managed to pull her down just as the large shape of an animal hurled itself across the place where she had been only seconds before. At the same time as pulling her down, he switched on his flashlight.

The shape shot past, but was still caught for an instant in the beam of Akimbo's flashlight. And it was long enough for all of them to realise that what had leapt past them was a leopard – a leopard that had now vanished into the darkness behind them.

For a moment nobody was able to speak. Then Jen dusted herself off and switched on her own flashlight. In the background, not far away, a few of the braver baboons had ventured out and were staring at the three unexpected visitors. A large baboon took a few steps forward, sniffed at the air, and then grunted. This seemed to calm the rest of the troop, who now stopped barking and howling.

'So that was what was going on,' said Jen. 'A leopard. Their most deadly enemy.'

She turned to Akimbo and shook his hand. 'You saved me there,' she said. 'That leopard would have mauled me badly if you hadn't pulled me to the ground.'

Akimbo did not know what to say – he did not think of himself as a hero. And it had all happened so quickly that he had not even thought about it. He had seen the sudden movement and he had realised that Jen was in danger; his reactions had done the rest.

They made their way back to their hut in silence. Akimbo was pleased that everything had worked out well. They had saved the baboons from their enemy, and at the same time Jen had not been hurt. It could have turned out very differently, of course, but he did not think about that. And soon they were back in the hut, safely back in their sleeping bags, with their fire burning bright, keeping them safe through the African night, safe until morning.

Lunchtime lesson

'The baboons will be very upset,' said Jen the next morning. 'Most of the time they can look after themselves, but leopards still take them. They go for the baboons on the edge of the troop and it's over pretty quickly, I'm afraid.'

Akimbo nodded. Having been brought up on the game reserve, he knew that these things happened in nature, but he still found it sad to think of it.

They were walking very quietly to a place near the hill where they would spend the day watching the baboons. Jen had explained that after the night's disturbances, the baboons would probably

31

stay close to home. It would be a day or two, she thought, before they started foraging for food again.

She was right. When they reached their destination, they could see the large baboons sitting on their rocks while down below them the youngsters played some game of their own.

'They love playing,' said Jen, as she set up her telescope under the shade of a tree. 'Look at those two over there.'

Akimbo and Kosi looked in the direction she was pointing. Two small baboons, not much bigger than an ordinary cat, were pushing one another over in the dust. One seized the other's tail and gave it a sharp tug, while the other spun round and tried to fend off his attacker with blows and nips. Then they struggled together in a bundle until another young baboon strolled across and distracted them.

'They have long friendships,' Jen explained, as she peered through the lens of her telescope. 'And they live in families.'

'Just like us?' asked Akimbo.

'Yes,' said Jen. 'Just like us. But a bit different.

You see that group over there, where the little ones are playing. I'm pretty sure that's a family. But it's mostly females and children; the males are sitting together over there. Do you see them?'

She beckoned the boys over to the telescope and invited them to look through it. Akimbo went first. He saw a group of large baboons sitting near a flat rock. They were peering out over the top of the grass, as if keeping guard.

'They're on sentry duty,' Jen explained. 'They'll be looking out for that leopard, or for any other threat for that matter. They've seen us, but I think they know that we're all right.'

'Will they remember that we scared the leopard off?' asked Kosi.

'They might,' said Jen. 'They're very intelligent creatures after all. But it's always difficult to tell what an animal is thinking. You mustn't imagine that they think the same way as we do.'

'But you said they had friends,' Akimbo pointed out.

'Yes,' Jen said. 'They do. So I suppose they feel

fondness for others. Look over there. That's how they show it.'

She pointed to a small group of baboons that were sitting near the playing youngsters. It was Kosi's turn with the telescope now, and as he trained it on the baboons he let out a little exclamation. 'She's combing her friend's hair!' he said. 'Look! She's using her fingers as a comb.'

'That's called grooming,' said Jen. 'They'll do that for hours and hours. They love it. And it's how baboons make friends for life.'

For the next few hours, the boys sat with Jen under the tree while she busied herself making notes in her notebook. They did not have much to do, but every so often she asked them to count the number of baboons in a group while she wrote the results down. It was not very exciting for Akimbo and Kosi, but Jen explained that there was always a lot of watching in science and the fun would come later. 'The fun always comes,' she said. 'Believe me.'

And it did. Some hours later, just when Akimbo thought that the baboons would do nothing that day, two of them suddenly detached themselves from the others and started to edge their way towards the small group of people under the tree.

'Don't frighten them,' whispered Jen. 'Just let them come.'

The baboons inched forward and then stopped and sat down. Silently they stared at the people, looking at them as if they were trying to make out what on earth these strange creatures could be doing under the tree. Then they took a few steps closer, very casually, as if they wanted to give the impression that they were just going for an afternoon stroll. Having come a little closer, they would sit down and stare again.

After a while, the two visiting baboons were very close. Now it was possible for Akimbo and Kosi to study their expressions more closely. This made the baboons open their eyes wide at them, as if they were making faces. Jen smiled at this.

'They're trying to tell you something,' she whispered to the boys. 'They're trying to tell you that this is their place and you should have asked first before you came here. That's what all that means.'

Then it happened, and it happened so quickly that neither Akimbo nor Kosi had the time to stop it. They had been eating their lunch, which consisted of two large sandwiches Jen had made for them. When the two baboons had started to approach, the boys had put their sandwiches down on the grass so that they could finish them off later. Or that's what they thought; the baboons had something quite different in mind.

With a sudden whooping sound, the baboons dashed forward and snatched the sandwiches. Then, as quickly as they had darted in, they scampered off to a safe distance. Then they sat down, and watching the boys as they did so, they stuffed the half-eaten sandwiches into their mouths.

'Our lunch!' wailed Akimbo indignantly.

Jen laughed. 'Sorry about that,' she said. 'But it's a lesson that I also had to learn when I first got to know these animals. They love to steal.'

'But it's not fair,' said Kosi crossly. He still felt hungry and the only food was back at the hut.

'The baboons think it's perfectly fair,' said Jen. 'They were hungry; they saw some sandwiches. It was as simple as that.'

Akimbo and Kosi looked at one another. Jen was right, and they both decided that the best thing to do was to laugh. After all, it had been rather funny, and the baboons looked very pleased with themselves.

'All right then,' called out Akimbo. 'I hope you enjoyed that.'

The two baboons stared at them. Their mouths

were still full of the boys' lunch, and so they did not say anything in reply.

Akimbo turned to Jen. 'Did you notice something about the smaller one?' he asked.

Jen nodded. 'Yes, I think I did. He was limping, wasn't he?'

'Yes,' said Akimbo. 'It was his left back paw. It was really swollen.'

'Perhaps the leopard bit him,' said Kosi. 'Or slashed him with her claws.'

'Maybe,' said Jen. 'But it hasn't made him any the less brave, has it?'

Tommy and Ben

Over the next few days, the baboons settled down and began to range further in search of food. Not all of them went off on these expeditions, the mothers and the very young baboons remaining behind. Jen was quite happy to stay and watch them. She sat under her tree, looking through her telescope or binoculars, noting down what was happening among the rocks and trees where the troop lived.

'I'm just getting to know them now,' she explained to the boys. 'I'll come back and watch them later this year. I'll spend longer with them then.'

She was now trying to work out who was who in the troop. As she identified the baboons, she gave them each a name. To the leader of the troop, a large male with a deep, rather angry bark she had given the name Hobo, but she allowed the boys to choose names for some of the others. Akimbo selected the names for the two baboons who had stolen their sandwiches. He called them Tommy and Ben, after two boys in his class at school. Ben was the baboon with a limp.

'They're both a little bit greedy,' he said, smiling. 'Just like those two baboons.'

Jen laughed at the joke. 'All right,' she said. 'Tommy and Ben it is!'

If Tommy and Ben – the baboons – were greedy, then they were also very inquisitive. A couple of days after their first encounter with them, the two baboons started to take an interest in what was happening under the tree and decided to pay their watchers a visit. This time there was no food for them to steal, but that did not dampen their curiosity. This time they came even closer, so that they were almost within touching distance of the boys and Jen.

Akimbo took the chance to look at Ben's swollen foot. He had been right: it was almost twice the size of the baboon's other foot, and there was a dark bit behind the fur which looked as if blood had oozed out.

'It doesn't look too good,' he whispered to Jen. 'Look. It seems painful when he puts his weight on it.'

'Anything could have happened,' said Jen. 'If we hadn't seen him limping a few days ago I would have thought that he might have been stung by a scorpion – baboons are always teasing scorpions and get stung for their pains. But the swelling from a sting would have gone down by now.'

Akimbo peered more closely at Ben, who looked back at him with undisguised interest. Then he saw it, and he tugged at Jen's sleeve to get her attention.

'Look,' he said. 'Look, there's a piece of wire!'

He had been able to see the wire when Ben

changed the way he was sitting and stretched out his swollen leg. Now it was very visible, and there was no mistaking what it was.

'Ah!' said Jen. 'So that's what it is. Poor thing – he must be in terrible pain from it. It's twisted round his leg there, you see, and cut into his flesh.'

The thought of the pain which Ben must have been experiencing made Akimbo wince. 'We have to help him, Jen,' he said. 'We can't let him suffer.'

Jen frowned. 'I don't like the thought of him suffering either,' she said. 'But I'm not sure what we can do. We wouldn't be able to grab hold of him and take it off. He'd bite us badly if we tried that.'

Kosi had an idea. 'Couldn't we knock him out with one of those special darts the rangers use,' he said. 'Then, while he's asleep, we could deal with it.'

'A good idea,' said Jen. 'But I'm afraid that I don't have one of those special darts. So . . .'

'But you do have a net,' said Akimbo. 'You have that mosquito net that you put over your sleeping bag at night.'

Jen looked doubtful. 'Do you think that we could catch him with that? I'm not so sure.'

'But we could,' said Akimbo. 'We know how greedy he is. If we brought some food down here, he'd be bound to try to get it. And then we could throw the net over him . . .'

'And hold him down while Akimbo cuts the wire off his foot,' interjected Kosi.

'Yes,' said Akimbo. 'That's what we could do. Please, Jen, let's have a try.'

Jen took a bit more persuading, but at last she agreed that they could try the boys' plan.

'I don't think it'll do my mosquito net much good,' she said ruefully. 'But I suppose that it's more important to help poor Ben.'

The next day, they went down to their place under the tree early and tied the net on to one of the overhanging branches. When the piece of string holding the net up was released, it fell down like a billowing white cloud and covered whatever was beneath it. They tried it with Kosi, who pretended to be Ben for the trial. It worked perfectly, covering the boy with folds of material and making it impossible for him to move very much.

'But remember that Ben has got much bigger teeth than Kosi,' Jen warned. 'And he'll not be afraid to use them either.'

Akimbo knew that they would have to be very

careful. Fortunately Jen had
brought gloves with her, just in
case she had to handle a
baboon, and she said
that she would put these
on and hold the back of
Ben's head while Akimbo
took hold of the wire. Kosi
would try to grab his front
legs to stop him from scratching
anybody with those.

'It will be three against one,' said Akimbo.

'Or three against two,' warned Jen.

Akimbo was not sure what she meant, but she
soon explained. 'Baboons help one another,' she
said. 'Tommy will see what has happened and will
come to his aid. So that makes two of them.'

Akimbo had not thought of this. He looked
crestfallen. The possibility of another baboon
attacking them while they tried to deal with Ben
made the whole plan seem less likely to work.

'But don't worry,' said Jen brightly. 'I've had

an idea what we can do about that. Just listen to this.'

Akimbo and Kosi listened carefully as she explained what she had in mind. Then, rushing back to the hut, the two boys went to find the special things that she needed for her plan. It was a very funny plan, Akimbo thought, but it just might work.

Baboon rescue

When they returned to their observation post under the tree the next morning they were carrying much more than usual. Akimbo had the mosquito net, bundled up tightly but still rather heavy and unwieldy. Kosi was carrying a large bag of food, and Jen had a big tin of sticky molasses and a long pole.

Akimbo's mother had given them the molasses when they left the ranger station so that the boys could have it on their sandwiches. They both liked the sweet taste, and ever since they had arrived at the hut they had enjoyed it at every meal.

'Are you sure that baboons like molasses?' Akimbo asked, as they walked along the path to the hut. He was still a little bit doubtful as to whether Jen's plan would work, although she seemed confident enough.

'They love it,' she said. 'They can't resist it.'

At first Akimbo said nothing. He wanted the plan to work, but he saw so much that could go wrong with it. 'Let's hope,' he said. It was all he could think to say.

They continued with their walk and soon arrived at the tree. Akimbo dumped the net on the ground while Kosi, who was a good climber, scaled the trunk of the tree and edged slowly out along one of the overhanging branches. There he looped a piece of string round the branch so that both ends were hanging down by the ground. Then, while Akimbo tied one end of the string to the top of the net, Kosi climbed back down.

At first there was no sign of the baboons that morning.

'They're off looking for food,' said Jen. 'But don't worry – they'll come back. We'll just have to wait.'

Jen was right. After a few hours – hours which Akimbo thought dragged very slowly – the baboons returned. They knew that this was about to happen when they heard barking – those gruff barks that baboons exchange between one another. Then there were movements in the tall grass and dark shapes clambering up over rocks.

There was something that was exciting the baboons as they began to chatter and grunt once they reached the rocks. Then there was an indignant squealing sound, and two smaller baboons broke away from the group and ran over to anoth- er rock where they cowered, shrieking and baring their teeth at the others.

Jen watched this with interest. 'They've been punished for something,' she said to the boys. 'They're younger males, those two. Two boys. And they've been told off by a more senior male.'

'What did they do wrong?' asked Kosi.

Jen smiled. 'They probably didn't treat him with proper respect,' she said. 'Baboons have ranks, you know. There are the powerful and important, and then those who are not. The powerful remind the others from time to time of who's the boss!'

'It sounds a bit unfair,' said Akimbo. In fact, it sounded like bullying to him, but he knew that was the way that wild animals were. There was always somebody who was senior, and the junior ones had to remember this.

Now it was time to put out the food. Jen said that the baboons would smell the food if they put it out on the ground near the tree, and, with any luck Tommy and Ben would come over to investigate, as they had done the day before.

For an hour or so, nothing happened, and

Akimbo wondered whether the plan would work at all. Perhaps Tommy and Ben were not hungry, he thought. If they had been out to look for food, then maybe they had found some and would not be tempted by the smell of the human food.

It was Kosi who gave the warning. 'I think I can see something,' he whispered, tugging at Jen's sleeve. 'Look over there.'

What Kosi had seen was Tommy and Ben. The

two baboons had detached themselves from the rest and had made their way through the grass towards the observation post. Now they were just a short way away, and there was no doubt that they were interested in the food.

'I hope that Ben comes first,' whispered Akimbo. 'Come on, Ben! Delicious food!'

It was as if the baboon had heard him. Tommy remained sitting on the ground – he seemed a bit more nervous that Ben, even though he was the bigger of the two. Ben now moved forward, looking at the watching people from time to time, but clearly much more interested in the food which was lying on the ground directly beneath the branch of the large tree. And in the tree itself, suspended directly above the food, was the mosquito net.

Ben edged forward, gingerly, and Akimbo and the others held their breath in anticipation. Then, after a quick glance in the direction of the people, he reached forward to snatch the food.

That was Akimbo's signal to act. With a sharp tug on the string, he released the mosquito net. Down it fell, billowing folds of white cloth, like a large parachute – entirely over the surprised baboon below.

There was a tremendous howl from Ben, but he was well and truly caught in the folds of the net and was unable to run. Now Jen stepped forward and pulled the cloth tighter around him, binding him up in folds of white net. Ben screamed in fury, but his struggles only served to make the net tighter.

When the net fell upon Ben, Tommy jumped backwards in fright. But once his fright had been dispelled, he advanced towards the struggling bundle of cloth to see if he could help his friend. As he did so, he bared his fangs at the people to warn them off. It seemed as if he was saying: this is my friend, you keep away.

Now Jen gave a signal to Akimbo and the second part of the plan came into operation. At the end of the long pole was a sticky bundle of bread, secured by string. Akimbo now pushed this towards Tommy, who turned and stared at it suspiciously.

'Come on, Tommy,' muttered Akimbo. 'Lovely, sticky syrup!'

Naturally the baboon understood none of this, but he did realise that what he was being offered at the end of the pole was a treat that smelled more delicious than anything he had ever encountered before. Could he resist it?

No. He could not: it was just too much for any baboon, and he stretched forward and took the syrup-soaked lump of bread. Of course, this meant that his hands were soon covered with sticky substance, and this puzzled him. He started to lick at the syrup, found it delicious, and soon was completely absorbed in the task of getting the syrup off. Soon it was transferred to the fur on his face and below his jaws. It was all very confusing for him, even if it was also a very tasty thing.

With Tommy distracted in this way, Jen, with the help of the two boys, was able to extract Ben's damaged leg from the folds of the net. As she touched the injured flesh, the baboon gave a muffled howl from within the net. It was painful for him, but they had to do it, and with the help of a pair of pliers they had soon achieved what they set out to do.

Jen held up the cruel twist of wire once she and Akimbo had finished unwinding it. It was covered in blood and baboon hair. 'No wonder he was in pain,' she said. 'Look at that. It cut right into him.'

With their first aid complete, they unbundled the net and let Ben go free. It was not easy – he struggled and squealed a great deal – but eventually they got the net off him. Once that happened, he shot off at speed, dragging his injured leg behind him, stopping occasionally to lick at his wound. Tommy ran off with him, also stopping from time to time – in his case to lick not at a wound but at fur that was now completely covered in syrup.

Off track

They had only a few more days at the camp before they were due to go home. Nothing much happened in the baboon troop during this time, although one of the females gave birth one afternoon, and that created a lot of interest for the other baboons. It seemed as if the whole group wanted to welcome the new arrivals and crowded around to do so. Not everyone was allowed to get too close to the babies, though, although one or two of the mother's close friends were permitted to touch them. Jen noted all this down – she now knew just about all the members of the troop and knew, too, where they were in the pecking order.

On their last day at the observation post, there
was not much for the two boys to do. Jen was
watching the baboons and when Akimbo asked if
he and Kosi could go and explore on the other side
of the valley she saw no reason why they should
not. There had been no sign of any lions in the area
and it seemed safe enough, as long as they did not
go too far. Certainly there was very little chance of
their being surprised by a leopard – if there had
been any leopards nearby, the baboons would have
let them know by their behaviour.

The two boys set off, following the path of a

dried-up river bed. They saw monkeys in the trees at the edge of the river and a small family of warthogs, trotting through the bush with their tails erect, like little flagstaffs. But apart from that, it seemed as if any other animals were taking their afternoon rest.

They had walked for some distance when Akimbo noticed fresh ostrich tracks.

'We could follow these tracks,' he said to Kosi. 'Have you ever seen an ostrich close up?'

Kosi had not, and was keen on the idea. So together the two boys followed the tracks left in the ground by the large birds. Akimbo had been taught tracking by his father and was eager to put his skills to the test, and here, on the sandy soil of that part of the valley, it was not difficult to see the route that their quarry had taken.

Kosi was thrilled to be tracking with his friend. He listened carefully as Akimbo explained how a set of footprints could tell you so much. Some of the clues were simple, and seemed no more than common sense – if the soil disturbed by the animal's hoof or foot was still damp, then that meant that the creature had passed by very recently. That was very straightforward, and even somebody who had never tracked before could think of that.

But some of the things that Akimbo described were much more surprising. Kosi would never have thought that you could tell the speed at which an animal had been travelling merely by looking at its tracks in the sand. Yet you could and

Akimbo explained how.

'You see these tracks here,' he said to Kosi. 'They're far apart, aren't they? That means that the animal was running. It must have been in a hurry. And if you see them like that and then they suddenly turn, that means that they were being chased by something.'

These fascinating lessons continued for quite some time while the two boys walked past the end of the valley and on to a wide plain beyond. It was still possible to make out the ostrich tracks at the end of the valley, but when they reached the plain it was much more difficult.

'I think they must have gone that way,' said Akimbo, pointing in the direction of a clump of tall trees. Kosi nodded, but there was something in his friend's voice that sounded uncertain. Did Akimbo really know which way the birds had gone, or was he just guessing?

They walked for another hour or so before Akimbo stopped and sat down on a rock.

'I'm sorry,' he said. 'I've lost them. The ground here is too grassy.'

'It doesn't matter,' said Kosi, glancing up at the sun, now riding high in the sky. 'It's getting about time that we made our way back to the camp.'

Akimbo stood up, stretched, and looked around. 'Yes,' he said. 'It's about time.' And then he paused. When he had looked around, he had expected to know exactly which direction they would have to follow to get back to the camp. Now he found to his surprise that it was far from clear which way they would have to go.

He looked at Kosi, who returned his stare, shrugging his shoulders. 'I'm sorry,' Kosi said. 'I wasn't paying attention. I have no idea where we are.' He paused. 'Maybe we could follow our own tracks backwards.'

It was a good suggestion, but the moment that Akimbo looked down at the ground he knew that it would not be possible – it was one thing to follow tracks on sand, it was quite another to follow them on grass – in fact, it was impossible. And for the last half hour they had been on grass.

'Are we lost?' asked Kosi miserably.

Akimbo shook his head. 'I'm sure we came that way,' he said, pointing in the direction of a small granite hillock.

It did not seem familiar to Kosi, but he had no alternative but to trust his friend's instinct and to follow him.

They walked for hours. Once they arrived at the hillock, they realised that it was not the right place, and so they began to retrace their steps. Then Akimbo changed his mind and they went off in another direction.

Kosi was now worried. He had felt safe with his friend, but it was hard to feel confident when your friend kept changing his mind. And now, judging by the position of the sun and the length of the shadows, it was well past four o'clock in the afternoon. At six o'clock the skies would begin to darken and the night would fall. If they could not find their way by then, they would be out there in the bush at a time when wild animals would be on the prowl. Leopards. Lions. What chance would two small boys have against creatures like that?

Akimbo himself was now very worried. He imagined what Jen must be thinking, and he wondered what she would do. Would she try to find them, or would she make her way back by herself to the ranger camp and get his father to come to the rescue? Whatever happened, he would have to explain just how he had lost the way and he was sure that his father would think twice about letting him go out again by himself. That would be very hard to take.

Help!

When night falls in Africa it falls with suddenness. One moment the sky is blue and empty; the next it has faded and stars begin to appear. Then, as the last traces of light go from the sky there is nothing but darkness covering the land like a velvet cloth.

'We'll have to find somewhere safe to spend the night,' said Akimbo.

'If there *is* anywhere safe,' said Kosi. Looking around him, he could not see anywhere that looked like a good place to stay the night. There were no caves in the rocks, no trees with low branches on which they could lie, as if in a hammock.

Akimbo was looking too, and he, too, could see nothing. Yet they could hardly stay out there, unprotected from the dangers of the night.

'Maybe we could try shouting,' ventured Kosi. The suggestion did not sound very convincing, even to him, but he thought it was better than nothing. 'There may be some huts near here,' he added lamely. 'Or a ranger tent . . .'

Akimbo did not think that there was much point in shouting for help, but at least it amounted to doing something. So he looked out into the darkness, took a deep breath, and shouted *Help* at the top of his voice. Kosi did the same, and then the two of them stopped to listen. It would have been wonderful if an answering voice had come back, but there was nothing: just the faintest of echoes of their voices against the rocks of the hills – faint cries of *help* bouncing off the hard rock and then disappearing into the night air.

They repeated their cries again and again, each time with no result. And then, just when they were about to give up, they heard something.

'What was that?' asked Akimbo. He felt anxious: what if by shouting out they were merely giving away their position to some predator – perhaps to a lion?

The sound came again, and it was not the roar of a lion or the cough of a leopard: it was a barking sound.

Akimbo and Kosi stood stock still. A baboon! Then Akimbo shouted out again and, after a short delay, there again came an answering bark.

Akimbo had noted the direction from which

the bark had come. 'It was over there,' he whispered to Kosi. 'And it's not far away.'

Carefully the two boys made their way through the darkness, trying to avoid the thorn bushes and the other obstacles that lay in their way. They half-walked, half-ran, so keen were they to find the baboon. If this was one of the baboons from the troop, then all they would have to do was to follow it through the darkness until they reached their sleeping place. Once they found that, it would be simple to locate the observation post and their camp.

Suddenly Akimbo stopped. From a clump of bushes, there had come a grunt.

'What is it?' whispered Kosi, his heart hammering with fear within him. Leopards grunted, he knew, and if this was a leopard they had stumbled upon . . .

It was not a leopard. As the two boys stood there in fright, a dark shape emerged from the bushes – a baboon. And even in the darkness, the boys could make out something special about this baboon – it was limping.

'Ben!' whispered Akimbo, his heart giving a

leap of joy. It was like finding a friend again when you thought that all was lost.

The baboon stopped and seemed to stare at the boys for a while, as if sizing them up. Then he gave another grunt and began to amble off into the shadows with that curious loping way that baboons have of walking. Without saying anything to one another, the two boys began to follow him, keeping a respectful distance so as not to frighten him, but close enough to make sure that they did not lose sight of their rescuer.

They were much closer to the camp than they thought, and it was only thirty minutes or so later that they saw, in the darkness ahead of them, the pinprick of light that announced the presence of the camp.

'Thank you, Ben,' Akimbo called out, and then, closely followed by Kosi, he began to run towards the light.

Jen hugged both boys so tightly that they could hardly breathe.

'I was worried sick,' she said. 'I waited until the sun went down, and then I got ready to drive back to the ranger camp. But then I asked myself what would happen if you then turned up and discovered the camp empty. So I decided to wait until morning. Thank goodness I did.'

She fed the boys with delicious hot soup while they told her the story of their adventure.

'It was all my fault,' said Akimbo. 'I was trying to track ostriches and . . .'

Jen did not let him finish. 'Let's not worry

about whose fault it was,' she said. 'The important thing is that you're back safely. That's all that counts.'

Akimbo was relieved that he was not being scolded for what happened, but he felt, too, that he had learned a lesson about being out in the bush: never forget where you are; always take note of and remember the things you've walked past. In this way you will be able to use landmarks to make your way home. It was not a lesson that he would forget in a hurry.

They also told Jen about how Ben had saved them, and she listened very carefully to that.

'I'm not sure if he would have done that deliberately,' she said. 'Perhaps he just happened to be there. And then he happened to be coming home.'

Akimbo was silent. He knew that you should not make up feelings and thoughts for animals – the things they did usually had reasons that were entirely their own and had nothing to do with us. But he was sure, in his heart of hearts, that Ben

was repaying them for getting the wire off his leg –
he was sure of that. And just by looking at his
friend, Akimbo knew that Kosi thought the same
way.

The next day they packed up the camp and
prepared to leave the area. As they made their way
back to the waiting truck, Akimbo saw a small
group of baboons watching them from the low
branch of a tree. At that distance he could not
make out the features of any of the baboons, but
he was sure that one of them was Ben.

'Goodbye,' he said under his breath. 'And
thank you.'

The baboons watched. One of them raised a
hand. Was he waving
farewell, or was he just
brushing away a fly?

Akimbo decided
that he was waving.

Brilliant baboon facts

There are five types of baboon: the olive baboon, the chacma, the guinea (all found in different parts of Africa), the hamadryas and the yellow baboon, both found in Africa but also in Arabia. The two most common are the olive and the yellow baboons, the smallest is the guinea and the largest is the hamadryas.

Baboons are known to be 'dog-faced' and have muzzles. They are from the primate family, and so are different from monkeys as they don't have tails.

Baboons live on the ground and are omnivorous, which means they eat everything – from grass to small antelopes! They have been known to raid human villages for food. They also have a bit of a sweet tooth and like foraging sweet gum from the bark of fever trees.

Normally waking up between seven and eight in the morning, baboons will descend from the trees and groom one another while the younger ones play.

In ancient Egypt the baboon was an important religious symbol – strange considering none are native to Egypt.

Scientists have discovered that despite not being part of the same genetic family as human beings, baboons are in fact very similar to us in the way that they can socially interact, with their group sustained by a strict hierarchy and rules.

The collective noun for baboons is either 'troop' or 'congress'.

Baboons have over thirty ways of communicating to one another using their voices, and like us they use gestures as well – including yawning to show their teeth as an act of aggression. Some people argue that we do that too, so maybe it's not just because you're tired!

In the wild, the average lifespan of a baboon is between twenty and thirty years, but in captivity they can live a lot longer.

As a means of protecting themselves from predators – the most threatening of whom is human – baboons will sleep in high trees and cliffs. They are also often hunted by leopards, lions, cheetahs and wild dogs, although their size (particularly the hamadryas) can make them formidable opponents!

Baboons can travel up to six miles a day moving in an organized unit, fanning out to feed and forage for food to bring back to their base.

Baboons also mourn the loss of their friends and family. According to one report, when a baboon was killed on a road in eastern Uganda the congress surrounded the female's body and refused to move for half an hour! Another reported seeing baboons throwing sticks and stones at passing cars after the death of one of their young on a road.

Despite their sympathetic reactions to traumatic events, they can still get pretty nasty! Male baboons don't take kindly to intruders and will often fight each other for dominance over the females.

Baboons exist as a large population, because, like us, they are extremely adaptable and can weather most conditions – and are obviously not shy of stealing an odd goat or two from their human neighbours. They mostly prefer savannahs and dry places, but some do live in the rainforests.

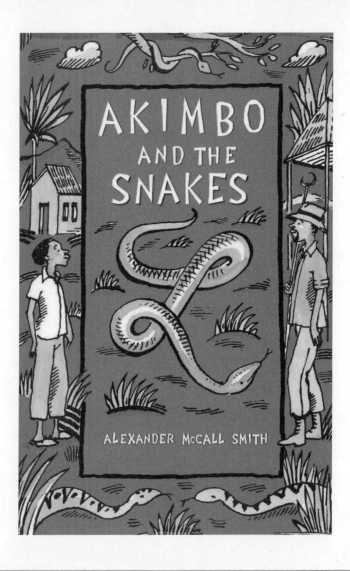